ni hao, kai-lan

Playdate with Lulu

adapted by Irene Kilpatrick
based on the screenplay "Lulu Day" written by Bradley Zweig
illustrated by The Artifact Group

Ready-to-Read

Simon Spotlight/Nickelodeon
New York   London   Toronto   Sydney

Based on the TV series *Ni Hao, Kai-lan!*™ as seen on Nick Jr.®

SIMON SPOTLIGHT
An imprint of Simon & Schuster Children's Publishing Division
1230 Avenue of the Americas, New York, New York 10020
© 2010 Viacom International Inc. All rights reserved. NICKELODEON, *Ni Hao, Kai-lan!*, and all
related titles, logos, and characters are trademarks of Viacom International Inc.
All rights reserved, including the right of reproduction in whole or in part in any form.
SIMON SPOTLIGHT, READY-TO-READ, and colophon are registered trademarks of
Simon & Schuster, Inc.
For information about special discounts for bulk purchases, please contact Simon & Schuster
Special Sales at 1-866-506-1949 or business@simonandschuster.com.
Manufactured in the United States of America
1109 LAK
2 4 6 8 10 9 7 5 3
Library of Congress Cataloging-in-Publication Data
Kilpatrick, Irene.
Playdate with Lulu / adapted by Irene Kilpatrick ; based on a teleplay by Bradley Zweig ;
illustrated by The Artifact Group. — 1st ed.
p. cm. — (Ready-to-read)
"Based on the TV series Ni Hao, Kai-lan as seen on Nickelodeon"—Copyright p.
ISBN 978-1-4169-9089-5
I. Zweig, Bradley. II. Artifact Group. III. Ni Hao Kai-lan (Television program) IV. Title.
PZ7.K5592Pl 2010
[E]—dc22
2009023723

Ni hao! I am .
KAI-LAN

My friend is coming
LULU

to play today.

will be here soon.
LULU

I made a PINWHEEL for LULU.

Do you know how

to make a PINWHEEL spin?

You blow, blow, blow at it.

Look, there is !
LULU

 always flies with her
LULU

big  .
RED BALLOON

We are ready to play!

I like this .
PIRATE HAT

I want to play pirates!

 likes the .
LULU   TEAPOT

She wants to play .
TEA PARTY

Uh-oh! What can we do?
We need to find something
we both want to play!

I want to play with the .

HOOPS

LULU wants to play with

the GLITTER.

Uh-oh! What can we do?

We need to find something

we both want to play!

I want to blow big .
BUBBLES

 wants to dance.
LULU

We have to try
to find the reason why
we cannot figure out
what to play together!

LULU wanted to play with the TEAPOT and the GLITTER.
I wanted to play with the PIRATE HAT and the HOOPS.

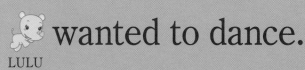 wanted to dance.

I wanted to blow big .

We want to do

different things!

I see 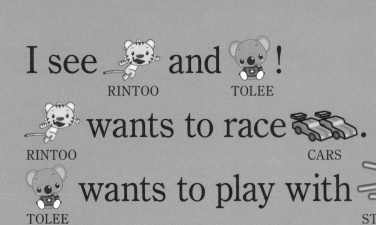 and !
RINTOO   TOLEE

wants to race .
RINTOO   CARS

wants to play with .
TOLEE   STICKS

They want to play with
different things!
What can they do?

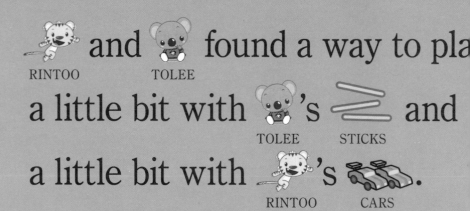 and  found a way to play

RINTOO   TOLEE

a little bit with 's ≥ and

TOLEE   STICKS

a little bit with 's 🚗.

RINTOO   CARS

TOLEE is making a CITY

with his STICKS.

RINTOO will race his CARS down

the STREET of the CITY!

 and  found a way

RINTOO   TOLEE

to play a little bit

of what they both

wanted to do.

and I can do that too!
LULU

We can have a pirate .
TEA PARTY

LULU can throw ✦ on my 〰
GLITTER   HOOP

It is a super sparkly ✦ 〰!
                    GLITTER HOOP

LULU can do a BUBBLE dance
while I blow BUBBLES.

We can play different things
and still play together!

We can play a little bit
of what we both want to do!

I wish  and I could play
LULU
together every day!

Today was a

super special playdate!